Ryan Matteo

W9-BRB-412

Chipmunk at Hollow Tree Lane

SMITHSONIAN'S BACKYARD

For Natalie with love from Mom.
    —V.S.

I dedicate this book to the
little furry animals inside all of us.
    —A.D.

Copyright © 1994 by Trudy Management Corporation,
165 Water Street, Norwalk, CT 06856, and the Smithsonian Institution, Washington, DC 20560.

All rights reserved. No part of this book may be reproduced or transmitted in any form or by any means
whatsoever without prior written permission of the publisher.

Book Design: Shields & Partners, Westport, CT

First Edition
10 9 8 7 6 5 4 3
Printed in Singapore

Acknowledgements:
    Our very special thanks to Dr. Charles Handley of the department of vertebrate zoology at the
Smithsonian's National Museum of Natural History for his curatorial review.

Library of Congress Cataloging-in-Publication Data

Sherrow, Victoria.

Chipmunk at Hollow Tree Lane / by Victoria Sherrow ;
illustrated by Allen Davis.
        p.   cm.
Summary: Describes how Chipmunk gathers and stores food to prepare for winter.
        ISBN 1-56899-028-6
1. Chipmunks — Juvenile fiction. [1. Chipmunks — Fiction.]
I. Davis, Allen, ill. II. Title.
        PZ10.3.S387Ch 1994   93-27267
        [E] — dc20   CIP
                                              AC

Chipmunk at Hollow Tree Lane

by Victoria Sherrow
Illustrated by Allen Davis

Soundprints

A Division of Trudy Management Corporation, Norwalk, Connecticut

One November morning, sunshine lights up the big backyard behind the blue house on Hollow Tree Lane. Under the shadow of a maple tree, Chipmunk peeks out of the hole of her underground burrow at the yard's edge. The air feels chilly because winter is coming soon. Chipmunk climbs out of her burrow. It is time to get to work!

4

She scampers through crisp golden leaves scattered over the yard. In the summer there were many strawberries, blueberries, and blackberries to eat. Chipmunk stored some of their seeds for the long winter ahead. Now all these juicy berries are gone.

Suddenly, Chipmunk comes upon a bush with some small, dark red berries left on it. *"Ch-ch-i-i-ip-pp!"* She trills with excitement. These are viburnum berries with delicious seeds that can be saved for winter meals. Chipmunk must hurry. The birds in the yard like these berries, too.

Her little jaws munch away on the berries. Chewing faster and faster, she drops the berry peels onto the ground. Only the seeds will keep all winter long. Chipmunk stuffs the seeds inside her striped cheeks where they are safely carried in special pouches. Her cheeks stretch like balloons as she adds more seeds.

Finding no more berries, Chipmunk runs back to her burrow. She scurries down the tunnel. In her burrow is a fluffy nest of dried grass and leaves. Buried underneath the nest, in a secret hiding place, are other seeds and nuts that Chipmunk has been gathering all summer and fall.

With her front paws, Chipmunk pushes aside the leaves and grass that cover the stored food. She quickly empties her cheek pouches and adds these new seeds to the others.

Then she climbs back outside to look for more food. She stops near the woods on the other side of the yard. There she spies acorns among the fallen leaves under an oak tree.

Just as Chipmunk reaches for a nut, she hears a loud squawk above her.

Chipmunk darts under the edge of a big rock, safe from danger. A cold wind ripples through the tree branches as she waits. Chipmunk peers out from beneath the rock.

"*Caw! Caw!*" A big black crow lands on the dry leaves. He pecks at the ground looking for food.

After the crow flies away, Chipmunk scrambles back into the open to gather acorns. She reaches for one nut, then another, until she has crammed three acorns inside each cheek.

She races back to her burrow to hide these nuts. Within minutes, she climbs back out again. There are more nuts to gather, and winter will soon be here.

Under the oak tree, Chipmunk fills her cheek pouches once again. As she works, another chipmunk scurries toward the tree.

Chipmunk hops up onto a rock and looks fierce. *"Chip!-chip!-chip!"* she shouts as her tail thumps up and down. This is a warning to the stranger to go away!

Sitting up on his hind legs, the other chipmunk listens, then turns and runs into the woods.

Chipmunk goes back to work, carrying acorns from the oak tree to her burrow. By now, she is hungry. She stops long enough to eat two of her acorns and a plump pink worm.

Late afternoon sunshine flickers through the tree branches, casting lacy shadows on the ground. Chipmunk searches carefully for one last load of food. By sunset, she is ready for a good night's sleep.

Tomorrow she will leave her burrow again. She will find no more seeds or nuts to gather.

As the days turn frosty and the earth hardens, Chipmunk stays in her burrow on her soft, cozy nest, safe from the December snow and winds. Her thick winter coat gives her warmth.

Chipmunk spends most of the winter sleeping. From time to time, she awakens to munch on the food buried under her nest. Snug in her burrow, Chipmunk will wait for the warm spring sunshine. With it will come fresh green plants, tree buds, and other things good to eat in the backyard of the blue house on Hollow Tree Lane.

About the Chipmunk

The chipmunk depicted in this story is the eastern chipmunk, found throughout New England, the central Atlantic region, and much of the midwestern United States. Eastern chipmunks are larger than western chipmunks, measuring about 10 inches and weighing about 3.5 ounces. They can run and climb rapidly, and can even swim. Staying in one burrow all their lives, they sometimes add extra tunnels and rooms. Nuts, seeds and other types of vegetation make up their main diet, as well as some invertebrates such as worms, slugs, and snails. Chipmunks have dry cheek pouches to carry food to their nests. These pouches stretch to carry amazing numbers of seeds — three or four thousand in some cases!

Glossary

acorn: a type of nut found on oak trees.

burrow: a hole in the ground that an animal digs to use as a home.

crow: a large bird with shiny black feathers, known for its loud "caw".

pouch: a pocket-like container used for holding and carrying items.

viburnum berry: the red or black fruit appearing in late summer and autumn on the viburnum bush, which is found mostly in the eastern United States.

Points of Interest in this Book

pp. 4-5, 14-15 daisy.
pp. 6-7 gypsy mushroom.
pp. 6-7, 22-23, 24-25 white pinecone.
pp. 12-13, 14-15 viburnum berries.
pp. 12-13, 14-15, 28-29 sunflower seeds, grass seeds, white oak and pin oak acorns.

pp. 16-17 American toad, toadstool.
pp. 16-17, 20-21 white oak acorns.
pp. 18-19 beefsteak mushroom.
pp. 18-19, 24-25 wild strawberry (jagged-leafed plant).
pp. 22-23 turkey tail fungus.
pp. 24-25 sarsaparilla (green bulbous plant).